HURRY UP, ALFIE!

For Anna Vivas and Rafi

CLARION BOOKS
3 Park Avenue, New York, New York 10016

Copyright © 2015 by Anna Walker

First published by Scholastic Press, a division of Scholastic Australia
Pty Limited, in 2015. First published in the United States in 2016.
This edition is published under license from Scholastic Australia Pty Limited.

Clarion Books is an imprint of Houghton Mifflin Harcourt Publishing Company.

www.hmhco.com

The illustrations in this book were executed in ink and collage.
The text was set in Chaparral and Chaloops Medium.

Library of Congress Cataloging-in-Publication Data.
Names: Walker, Anna. • Title: Hurry up, Alfie! / by Anna Walker.
Description: Boston ; New York : Clarion Books, Houghton Mifflin Harcourt, 2016.
"First published by Scholastic Press, a division of Scholastic Australia Pty Limited, in 2015."
Summary: "It's time to get dressed and go the park, but Alfie is still in his pajamas. Putting
on clothes seems like the least appealing thing to do for this energetic and curious little
alligator, especially when there are so many amusing distractions"—Provided by publisher.
Identifiers: LCCN 2015020005 | ISBN 9780544586543 (hardback)
Subjects: | CYAC: Mother and child—Fiction. | Morning—Fiction. | Clothing and dress—
Fiction. | Alligators—Fiction. | BISAC: JUVENILE FICTION / Animals / Alligators &
Crocodiles. | JUVENILE FICTION / Imagination & Play. | JUVENILE FICTION /
Clothing & Dress. | JUVENILE FICTION / Humorous Stories.
Classification: LCC PZ7.W15214 Hu 2016 | DDC [E]—dc23
LC record available at http://lccn.loc.gov/2015020005

Manufactured in Malaysia
TK 10 9 8 7 6 5 4 3 2 1
45XXXXXXX

HURRY UP, ALFIE!

by ANNA WALKER

CLARION BOOKS
Houghton Mifflin Harcourt • Boston New York

Good morning, Alfie. It's time to get up.
The sun is shining and we have a busy day!

Alfie's not here.

Oh, that's a pity. I thought Alfie might like to come
to the park with me. Bert will be there . . .

Alfie's here!

Let's get ready to go.

How about you get dressed and *then* you show me your handstand?

Alfie, *now* what are you doing?

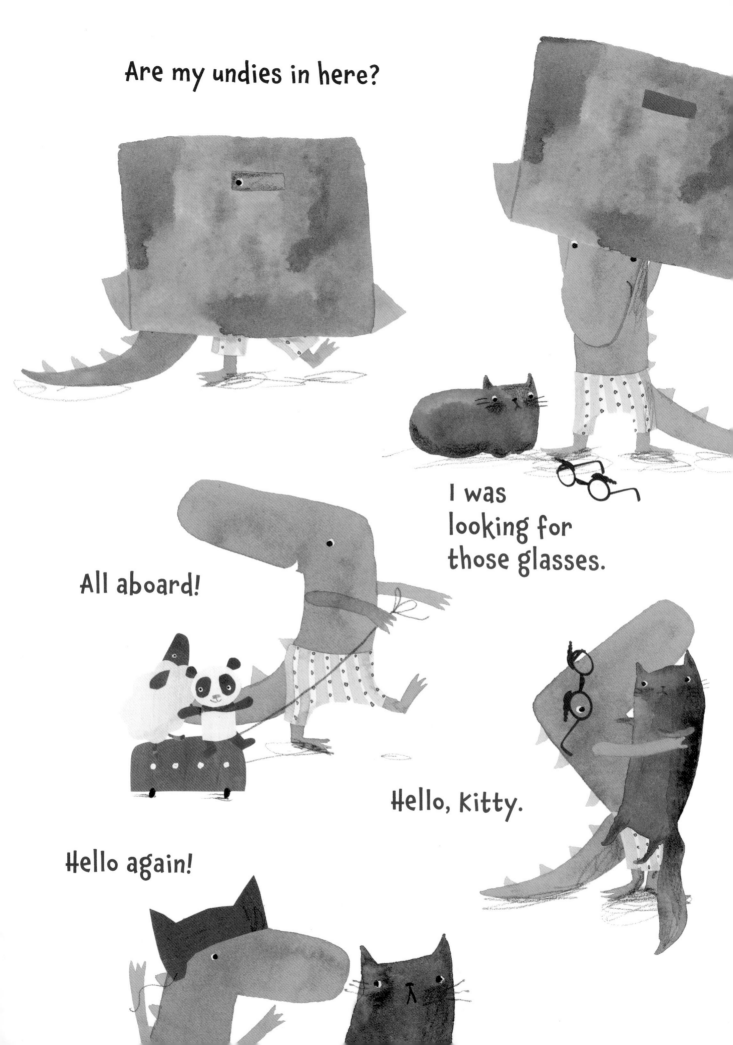

Look out, Kitty!

Alfie, we really have to go.

I'm ready!

Alfie! You don't need your umbrella. You need your clothes!